MOTHER GOOSE

KEEPSAKE COLLECTION

sequoia
children's publishing

Old MacDonald

Illustrated by Tammie Lyon

Old MacDonald had a farm, E-I-E-I-O
And on his farm he had some cows, E-I-E-I-O
With a moo-moo here and a moo-moo there,
Here a moo, there a moo, everywhere a moo-moo
Old MacDonald had a farm, E-I-E-I-O

Old MacDonald had a farm, E-I-E-I-O
And on this farm he had some donkeys, E-I-E-I-O
With a hee-haw here and a hee-haw there,
Here a hee, there a haw, everywhere a hee-haw
Old MacDonald had a farm, E-I-E-I-O

Old MacDonald had a farm, E-I-E-I-O
And on this farm he had some pigs, E-I-E-I-O
With an oink-oink here and an oink-oink there,
Here an oink, there an oink, everywhere an oink-oink
Old MacDonald had a farm, E-I-E-I-O

Old MacDonald had a farm, E-I-E-I-O
And on this farm he had some ducks, E-I-E-I-O
With a quack-quack here and a quack-quack there,
Here a quack, there a quack, everywhere a quack-quack
Old MacDonald had a farm, E-I-E-I-O

Little Bo-Peep

Illustrated by Sharon Cartwright

Little Bo-Peep has lost her sheep,
And can't tell where to find them.
Leave them alone,
And they'll come home,
Wagging their tails behind them.

Little Boy Blue

Illustrated by Sharon Cartwright

Little Boy Blue,
Come blow your horn.
The sheep's in the meadow,
The cow's in the corn.

Baa, Baa, Black Sheep

Illustrated by Thea Kliros

Baa, baa, black sheep
Have you any wool?
Yes sir, yes sir,
Three bags full:
One for the master,
One for the dame,
And one for the little boy
Who lives down the lane.

Mary Had a Little Lamb

Illustrated by Thea Kliros

Mary had a little lamb,
Its fleece was white as snow.
And everywhere that Mary went
The lamb was sure to go.

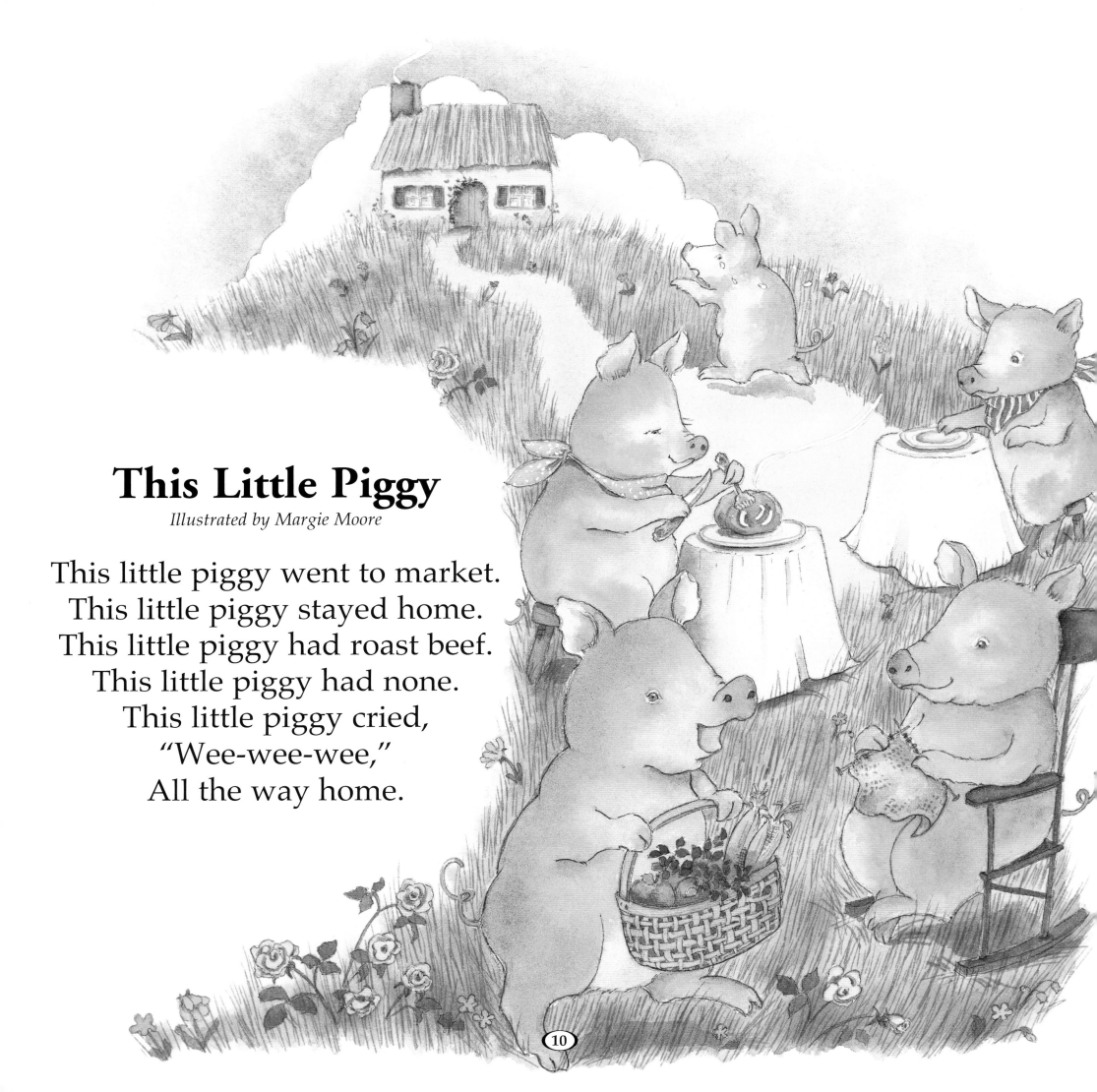

This Little Piggy

Illustrated by Margie Moore

This little piggy went to market.
This little piggy stayed home.
This little piggy had roast beef.
This little piggy had none.
This little piggy cried,
"Wee-wee-wee,"
All the way home.

Three Blind Mice

Illustrated by Margie Moore

Three blind mice. Three blind mice.
See how they run, see how they run!
They all ran after the farmer's wife,
Who cut off their tails with a carving knife.
Have you ever seen such a sight in your life,
As three blind mice?

Sing a Song of Sixpence

Illustrated by Kathleen O'Malley

Sing a song of sixpence,
A pocket full of rye;
Four-and-twenty blackbirds
Baked in a pie!

When the pie was opened,
The birds began to sing!
Wasn't that a dainty dish
To set before the king?

Little Robin Redbreast

Illustrated by Kathleen O'Malley

Little Robin Redbreast
Sat upon a tree.
Up went Pussycat;
Down went he.
Down came Pussycat;
Away Robin ran.
Says little Robin Redbreast,
"Catch me if you can!"

Hey, Diddle, Diddle

Illustrated by Marnie Webster

Hey, diddle, diddle,
The cat and the fiddle,
The cow jumped
Over the moon.
The little dog laughed
To see such sport,
And the dish ran away
With the spoon.

Pussycat, Pussycat

Illustrated by Marnie Webster

Pussycat, Pussycat, where have you been?
I've been to London to visit the Queen.
Pussycat, Pussycat, what did you there?
I frightened a little mouse under her chair.

My Dog Spot

Illustrated by Margie Moore

I have a white dog
Whose name is Spot,
And he's sometimes white
And he's sometimes not.
But whether he's white
Or whether he's not,
There's a patch on his ear
That makes him Spot.

He has a tongue
That is long and pink,
And he lolls it out
When he wants to think.
He seems to think most
When the weather is hot
He's a wise sort of dog,
Is my dog, Spot.

He likes a bone
And he likes a ball,
But he doesn't care
For a cat at all.
He waggles his tail
And he knows what's what,
So I'm glad that he's my dog,
My dog, Spot.

Where Has My Little Dog Gone?

Illustrated by Jeremy Tugeau

Oh where, oh where has my little dog gone?
Oh where, oh where can he be?
With his ears cut short and his tail cut long,
Oh where, oh where can he be?

I'm Just a Little Puppy

Illustrated by Jeremy Tugeau

I'm just a little puppy and as good as can be,
And why they call me naughty I'm sure I cannot see.
I've only carried off one shoe and torn the baby's hat,
And chased the ducks and spilled the milk—
there's nothing bad in that!

The Purple Cow

Illustrated by Betsy Day

I never saw a purple cow,
I hope I never see one;
But I can tell you anyhow,
I'd rather see than be one.

The Piper's Son

Illustrated by Betsy Day

Tom, Tom, the piper's son,
Stole a pig and away he run!
The pig thought it was quite a treat,
To be carried down the street.

Old Mother Goose

Illustrated by Sharon Cartwright

Old Mother Goose,
When she wanted to wander,
Would ride through the air
On a very fine gander.

Old Mother Hubbard

Illustrated by Sharon Cartwright

Old Mother Hubbard
Went to the cupboard
To give her poor dog a bone.

When she got there,
The cupboard was bare,
And so her poor dog had none.

Little Miss Muffet

Illustrated by Thea Kliros

Little Miss Muffet
Sat on a tuffet,
Eating her curds and whey.
Along came a big spider,
Who sat down beside her,
And frightened Miss Muffet away.

Little Miss Tucket

Illustrated by Thea Kliros

Little Miss Tucket
Sat on a bucket,
Eating some peaches and cream.
Along came a grasshopper
Who tried hard to stop her,
But she said,
"Go away, or I'll scream."

A Horse and a Flea

Illustrated by Susan Spellman

A horse and a flea and three blind mice
Met each other while skating on ice.
The horse he slipped and fell on the flea.
The flea said, "Oops, there's a horse on me!"

Fiddle-De-Dee

Illustrated by Susan Spellman

Fiddle-de-dee, Fiddle-de-dee,
The fly shall marry the bumblebee.
They went to church, and married was she;
The fly had married the bumblebee.

Cock-a-Doodle-Doo

Illustrated by Nan Brooks

Cock-a-Doodle-doo,
My dame has lost her shoe,
And master's lost his fiddling stick,
Sing doodle-doodle-doo.

The Cock Crows

Illustrated by Nan Brooks

The cock crows in the morn
To tell us to rise,
And he that lies late
Will never be wise:
For early to bed
And early to rise
Is the way to be healthy
And wealthy and wise.

29

The Donkey

Illustrated by Betsy Day

Donkey, donkey, old and gray,
Open your mouth and gently bray;
Lift your ears and blow your horn,
To wake the world this sleepy morn.

Lock and Key

Illustrated by Betsy Day

I am a gold lock.
I am a gold key.
I am a silver lock.
I am a silver key.
I am a brass lock.
I am a brass key.
I am a lead lock.
I am a lead key.
I am a don lock.
I am a don key.

Bell Horses

Illustrated by Jeremy Tugeau

Bell horses, bell horses,
What time of day?
One o'clock, two o'clock,
Three and away.

The Wise Old Owl

Illustrated by Jeremy Tugeau

A wise old owl sat in an oak.
The more he heard, the less he spoke;
The less he spoke, the more he heard.
Why aren't we all like that wise old bird?

Old King Cole

Illustrated by Thea Kliros

Old King Cole
Was a merry old soul,
And a merry old soul was he;
He called for his pipe,
And he called for his bowl,
And he called for his fiddlers three.

Jack Sprat

Illustrated by Thea Kliros

Jack Sprat could eat no fat.
His wife could eat no lean.
And so between them both, you see,
They licked the platter clean.

Humpty Dumpty

Illustrated by Margie Moore

Humpty Dumpty sat on a wall;
Humpty Dumpty had a great fall!
All the king's horses
And all the king's men
Couldn't put Humpty together again.

A Dozen Eggs

Illustrated by Margie Moore

I bought a dozen new-laid eggs
From good old Farmer Dickens.
I hobbled home upon two legs
And found them full of chickens.

Mary, Mary

Illustrated by Kathleen O'Malley

Mary, Mary, quite contrary,
How does your garden grow?
With silver bells and cockleshells,
And pretty maids all in a row.

Georgie Porgie

Illustrated by Kathleen O'Malley

Georgie Porgie, pudding and pie,
Kissed the girls and made them cry.
When the boys came out to play,
Georgie Porgie ran away.

Monday's Child

Illustrated by Linda Clearwater

Monday's child is fair of face,
Tuesday's child is full of grace,
Wednesday's child is full of woe,
Thursday's child has far to go,
Friday's child is loving and giving,
Saturday's child works hard for its living,
But the child that's born on the Sabbath day,
Is bonny and blithe, and good and gay.

Play Days

Illustrated by Linda Clearwater

How many days has my baby to play?
Saturday, Sunday, Monday,
Tuesday, Wednesday, Thursday, Friday;
Saturday, Sunday, Monday,
Hop away, skip away,
My baby wants to play.
My baby wants to play every day.

One, Two, Buckle My Shoe

Illustrated by Thea Kliros

One, two, buckle my shoe.
Three, four, knock at the door.
Five, six, pick up sticks.
Seven, eight, lay them straight.
Nine, ten, a good fat hen.

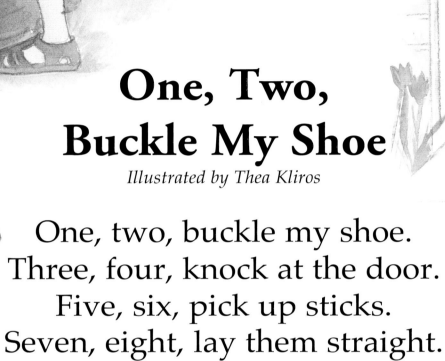

(42)

One for the Money

Illustrated by Thea Kliros

One for the money,
And two for the show,
Three to get ready,
And four to go.

Handy Pandy

Illustrated by Kathleen O'Malley

Handy Pandy, Jack-a-dandy,
Loves plum cake and sugar candy.
He bought some at a grocer's shop,
And out he came, hop, hop, hop.

Lucy Locket

Illustrated by Kathleen O'Malley

Lucy Locket lost her pocket,
Kitty Fisher found it;
Not a penny was there in it,
Only ribbon round it.

Miss Mackay

Illustrated by Kathleen O'Malley

Alas, alas, for Miss Mackay!
Her knives and forks have run away.
And where the cups and spoons are going,
She's sure there is no way of knowing.

Anna Elise

Illustrated by Wayne Parmenter

Anna Elise,
She jumped with surprise.
The surprise was so quick,
It played her a trick.
The trick was so rare,
She jumped in a chair.
The chair was so frail,
She jumped in a pail.
The pail was so wet,
She jumped in a net.
The net was so small,
She jumped on a ball.
The ball was so round,
She jumped on the ground.
And ever since then,
She's been turning around.

The Old Woman

Illustrated by Wayne Parmenter

The old woman stands at the tub, tub, tub,
The dirty clothes to rub, rub, rub;
But when they are clean and fit to be seen,
She'll dress like a lady and dance on the green.

My Little Brother

Illustrated by Linda Clearwater

Little brother, darling boy
You are very dear to me!
I am happy, full of joy,
When your smiling face I see.

How I wish that you could speak,
And could know the words I say!
Pretty stories I would seek
To amuse you every day.

Shake your rattle, here it is,
Listen to its merry noise!
And when you are tired of this,
I will bring you other toys.

My Little Sister

Illustrated by Linda Clearwater

I have a little sister,
She is only two years old,
But to us at home who love her,
She is worth her weight in gold.

We often play together,
And I begin to find,
That to make my sister happy,
I must be very kind.

I must not taunt or tease her,
Or ever angry be,
With the darling little sister,
That God has given to me.

49

Goober and I

Illustrated by Kathleen O'Malley

Goober and I were baked in a pie,
And it was wonderful hot.
We had nothing to pay
The baker that day
So we crept out and ran away.

Jack
Illustrated by Kathleen O'Malley

All work and no play makes
Jack a dull boy.
All play and no work makes
Jack a mere toy.

When Jack's a Very Good Boy
Illustrated by Kathleen O'Malley

When Jack's a very good boy,
He shall have cakes and custard;
But when he does nothing but cry,
He shall have nothing but mustard.

Little Jumping Joan

Illustrated by Wayne Parmenter

Here I am,
Little Jumping Joan.
When nobody's with me,
I'm all alone.

After Sunday

Illustrated by Wayne Parmenter

As Tommy Snooks and Bessy Brooks
Were walking out one Sunday,
Says Tommy Snooks to Bessy Brooks,
"Tomorrow will be Monday."

Betty Botter

Illustrated by Kathleen O'Malley

Betty Botter bought some butter,
But, she said, the butter's bitter;
If I put it in my batter,
It will make my batter bitter,
But a bit of better butter
Will make my batter better.
So she bought a bit of butter,
Better than her bitter butter,
And she put it in her batter
And the batter was not bitter.
So it was better Betty Botter bought
A bit of better butter.

Wee Willie Winkie

Illustrated by Kathleen O'Malley

Wee Willie Winkie
Runs through the town,
Upstairs and downstairs
In his nightgown,
Rapping at the window,
Crying through the lock,
"Are the children all in bed?
Now it's eight o'clock."

What Are Little Boys and Girls Made Of?

Illustrated by Linda Clearwater

What are little boys made of, made of?
What are little boys made of?
Snips and snails, and puppy-dogs' tails;
That's what little boys are made of, made of.

What are little girls made of, made of?
What are little girls made of?
Sugar and spice, and all things nice,
That's what little girls
are made of, made of.

Rain, Rain, Go Away

Illustrated by Linda Clearwater

Rain, rain, go away,
Come again another day;
Little Johnny wants to play.

Billy, Billy

Illustrated by Margie Moore

Billy, Billy, come and play,
While the sun shines bright as day.
Yes, my Polly, so I will,
For I love to please you still.
Billy, Billy, have you seen
Sam and Betsy on the green?
Yes, my dear I saw them pass,
Skipping over the new-mown grass.
Billy, Billy, come along,
And I will sing a pretty song.

Gregory Griggs

Illustrated by Margie Moore

Gregory Griggs, Gregory Griggs,
Had twenty-seven different wigs.
He wore them up, he wore them down,
To please the people of the town.
He wore them east, he wore them west,
And never could tell which one he liked best.

The Piper and His Cow

Illustrated by Yvette Banek

There was a piper who had a cow,
And he had nothing to give her;
He pulled out his pipes and played her a tune,
And asked the cow to consider.

The cow considered very well,
And gave the piper some money,
And asked him to play another tune,
That she would find quite funny.

The Hobbyhorse

Illustrated by Yvette Banek

I had a little hobbyhorse,
And it was dapple gray;
Its head was made of pea-straw,
Its tail was made of hay.

I sold it to an old woman
For a copper penny;
And I'll gladly sing my song again
If your horse should whinny!

Robert Barnes

Illustrated by Susan Spellman

Robert Barnes, fellow fine,
Can you shoe this horse of mine?
Yes, good sir, that I can,
As well as any other man.
There's a nail, and there's a prod,
And now, good sir, your horse is shod.

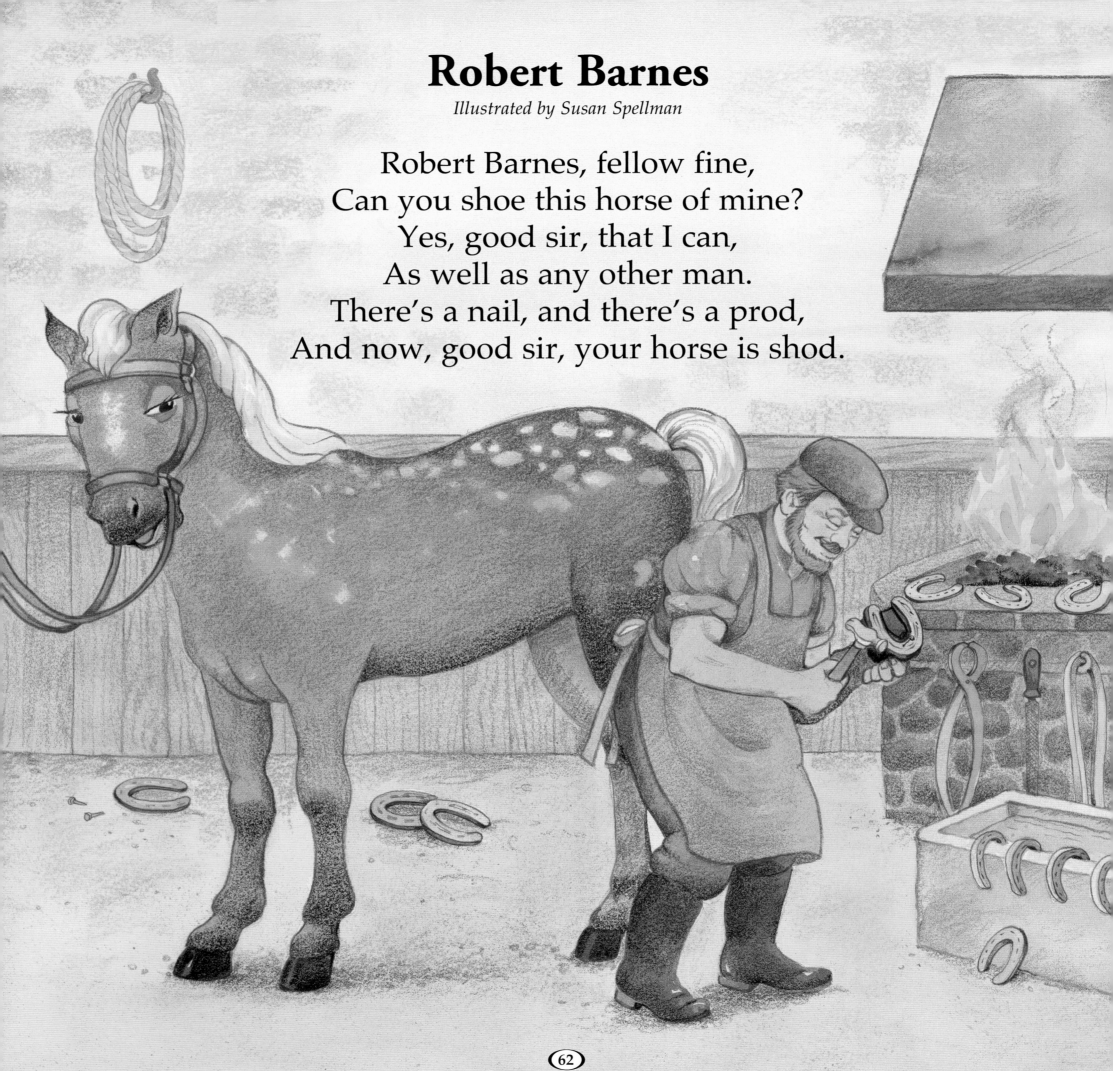

My Maid Mary

Illustrated by Susan Spellman

My maid Mary,
She minds the dairy,
While I go a-hoeing
And mowing each morn.
Gaily runs the reel
And the spinning wheel,
While I am singing
And mowing the corn.

The Boy in the Barn

Illustrated by Marnie Webster

A little boy went into a barn,
And lay down on some hay.
An owl came out and flew about,
And the little boy ran away.

The Little Mouse

Illustrated by Marnie Webster

I have seen you, little mouse,
Running all about the house,
Through the hole your little eye
In the wainscot peeping sly,
Hoping soon some crumbs to steal,
To make quite a hearty meal.
Look before you venture out,
See if kitty is about.

Harvesting

Illustrated by Jeremy Tugeau

The boughs do shake
And the bells do ring,
So merrily comes our harvest in,
Our harvest in, our harvest in,
So merrily comes our harvest in.

We've plowed, we've sowed,
We've reaped, we've mowed,
We've got our harvest in!

Old Soldier of Bister

Illustrated by Jeremy Tugeau

There was an old soldier of Bister,
Went walking one day with his sister,
When a cow at a poke
Tossed her into an oak
Before the old gentleman missed her.

Blue Bell Boy

Illustrated by Tammie Lyon

I had a little boy,
And called him Blue Bell;
Gave him a little work,
He did it very well.

I made him go upstairs
To bring me a gold pin;
In a coal bucket fell he,
Up to his little chin.

He went to the cellar
To draw a little chair;
And quickly did return
To say there was none there.

The Greedy Man

Illustrated by Tammie Lyon

The greedy man is he who sits
And bites bits out of plates,
Or else takes up a calendar
And gobbles all the dates.

Freddie and the Cherry Tree

Illustrated by Linda Clearwater

Freddie saw some fine ripe cherries
Hanging on a cherry tree.
And he said, "You pretty cherries,
Will you not come down to me?"

"Thank you kindly," said a cherry,
"We would rather stay up here;
If we ventured down this morning,
You would eat us up, I fear."

One, the finest of the cherries,
Dangled from a slender twig.
"You are beautiful," said Freddie,
"Red and ripe, and oh, how big!"

"Catch me," said the cherry, "catch me,
Little master, if you can."
"I would catch you very soon," said Freddie,
"If I were a grown-up man."

Freddie jumped and tried to reach it,
Standing high upon his toes;
But the cherry bobbed about,
And laughed, and tickled Freddie's nose.

"Never mind," said little Freddie,
"I shall have them when it's right."
But a blackbird whistled boldly,
"I shall have them all tonight."

There Was a Little Girl

Illustrated by Yvette Banek

There was a little girl,
who had a little curl,
Right in the middle of her forehead.
And when she was good,
she was very, very good,
But when she was bad, she was horrid.

She stood on her head,
on her little trundle bed,
With no one there to say, "No."
She screamed and she squalled,
she yelled and she bawled,
And drummed her little heels
against the window.

Her mother heard the noise,
and thought it was the toys,
Falling in the dusty attic.
She rushed up the flight,
and saw she was alright,
And hugged her most emphatic.

Moses' Toeses

Illustrated by Yvette Banek

Moses supposes his toeses are roses,
But Moses supposes erroneously.
For nobody's toeses are posies of roses
As Moses supposes his toeses to be.

Come Out to Play

Illustrated by Thea Kliros

Girls and boys,
Come out to play.
The moon doth shine
As bright as day.
Leave your supper,
And leave your sleep,
And come play with your playfellows
Into the street.

Willy Boy

Illustrated by Thea Kliros

Willy boy, Willy boy,
Where are you going?
I will go with you,
If that I may.

I'm going to the meadow
To see them a-mowing;
I'm going to help them
To make the hay.

Little Polly Flinders

Illustrated by Linda Clearwater

Little Polly Flinders
Sat among the cinders
Warming her pretty little toes;
Her mother came and stopped her,
For fear her lovely daughter
Would toast her pretty little nose.

Molly, My Sister

Illustrated by Linda Clearwater

Molly, my sister, and I fell out,
And what do you think it was all about?
She loved coffee and I loved tea,
And that was the reason
we couldn't agree.

Patience Is a Virtue

Illustrated by Linda Clearwater

Patience is a virtue,
Virtue is a grace,
Grace is a little girl
Who wouldn't wash her face.

There Was an Old Woman

Illustrated by Nan Brooks

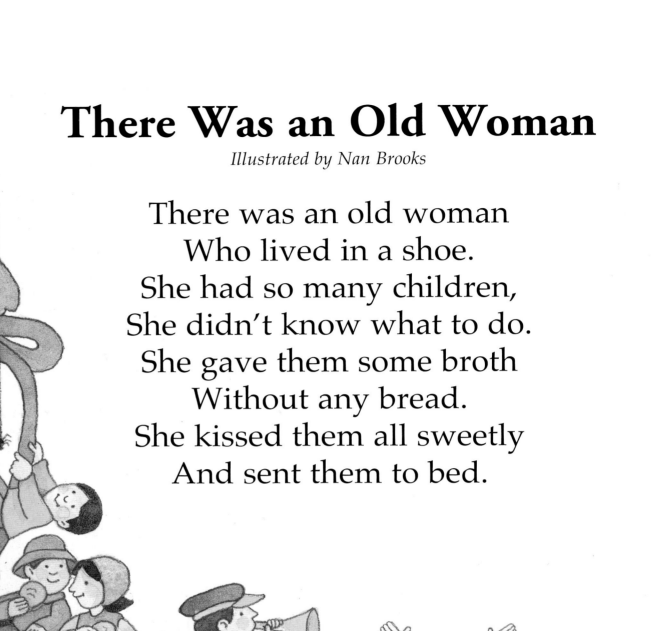

There was an old woman
Who lived in a shoe.
She had so many children,
She didn't know what to do.
She gave them some broth
Without any bread.
She kissed them all sweetly
And sent them to bed.

Peter Pumpkin-Eater

Illustrated by Nan Brooks

Peter, Peter, pumpkin-eater,
Had a wife and couldn't keep her.
He put her in a pumpkin shell,
And there he kept her very well.

Little Jack Horner

Illustrated by Marnie Webster

Little Jack Horner
Sat in a corner
Eating his Christmas pie;

He put in his thumb,
And pulled out a plum,
And cried,
"What a good boy am I!"

Pease Porridge Hot

Illustrated by Marnie Webster

Pease porridge hot,
Pease porridge cold,
Pease porridge in the pot
Nine days old.
Some like it hot,
Some like it cold,
Some like it in the pot,
Nine days old.

Rub-a-Dub-Dub

Illustrated by Jeremy Tugeau

Rub-a-dub-dub
Three men in a tub,
And how do you think they got there?
The butcher, the baker,
The candlestick maker,
They all jumped out of a rotten potato,
'Twas enough to make a man stare.

Peter Piper

Illustrated by Jeremy Tugeau

Peter Piper picked a peck
Of pickled peppers;
A peck of pickled peppers
Peter Piper picked.

If Peter Piper picked a peck
Of pickled peppers,
Where's the peck
of pickled peppers
Peter Piper picked?

Here We Go Round the Mulberry Bush

Illustrated by Thea Kliros

Here we go round the mulberry bush,
The mulberry bush, the mulberry bush,
Here we go round the mulberry bush,
On a cold and frosty morning.

Pat-a-Cake

Illustrated by Thea Kliros

Pat-a-cake, pat-a-cake,
Baker's man!
Bake me a cake,
As fast as you can.
Pat it, and prick it,
And mark it with a B.
Put it in the oven
For baby and me.

Twinkle, Twinkle, Little Star

Illustrated by Marnie Webster

Twinkle, twinkle, little star,
How I wonder what you are,
Up above the world so high,
Like a diamond in the sky.
Twinkle, twinkle, little star,
How I wonder what you are!

Roses Are Red

Illustrated by Marnie Webster

Roses are red,
Violets are blue,
Sugar is sweet,
And so are you!

Diddle, Diddle, Dumpling

Illustrated by Susan Spellman

Diddle, diddle, dumpling,
My son John,
Went to bed with his trousers on;
One shoe off, and one shoe on,
Diddle, diddle, dumpling,
My son John.

88

Sleepy Cat

Illustrated by Susan Spellman

The cat sat asleep
By the side of the fire.
The mistress snored loud as a pig.

John took up his fiddle,
By Jenny's desire,
And struck up a bit of a jig.

Sleep, Baby, Sleep

Illustrated by Wayne Parmenter

Sleep, baby, sleep.
Your father guards the sheep,
Your mother shakes
The dreamland tree,
And from it fall
Sweet dreams for thee.
Sleep, baby, sleep.

Hush-a-Bye

Illustrated by Wayne Parmenter

Hush-a-bye, baby,
Lie still with your daddy.
Your mommy has gone to the mill,
To get some meal to bake a cake.
So please, my dear baby, lie still.

Come, Let's to Bed

Illustrated by Yvette Banek

Come, let's to bed,
Says Sleepy-head.
Sit up awhile, says Slow.

Hang on the pot,
Says Greedy-gut,
We'll sup before we go.

To bed, to bed,
Cried Sleepy-head,
But all the rest said no!

It is morning now;
You must milk the cow,
And tomorrow to bed we go.

Sleep Tight

Illustrated by Yvette Banek

Goodnight,
Sleep tight,
Don't let the bedbugs bite.

Rock-a-Bye Baby

Illustrated by Linda Clearwater

Rock-a-bye, baby,
On the treetop.
When the wind blows,
The cradle will rock.
When the bough breaks,
The cradle will fall.
Down will come baby,
Cradle and all.